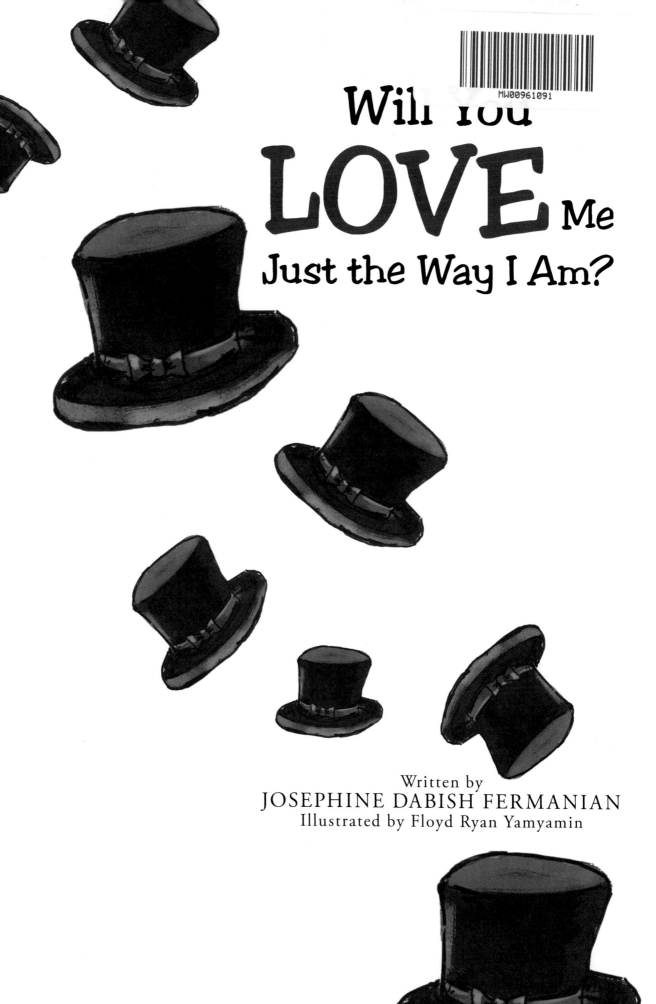

Will You LOVE Me Just the Way I Am?

Written by
JOSEPHINE DABISH FERMANIAN
Illustrated by Floyd Ryan Yamyamin

AuthorHouse™LLC
1663 Liberty Drive
Bloomington, IN 47403
www.authorhouse.com
Phone: 1-800-839-8640

Published by AuthorHouse 7/31/2014

ISBN: 978-1-4969-2394-3 (sc)
ISBN: 978-1-4969-2395-0 (e)

Library of Congress Conrol Number: TXU-1-878-853

Any people depicted in stock imagery provided by Thinkstock are models,
and such images are being used for illustrative purposes only.
Certain stock imagery © Thinkstock.

Because of the dynamic nature of the Internet, any web addresses or links contained in this book may have changed
since publication and may no longer be valid. The views expressed in this work are solely those of the author and do not
necessarily reflect the views of the publisher, and the publisher hereby disclaims any responsibility for them.

authorHOUSE®

There once was a hippo who
wanted to be loved. So she
went in search of love …

1

Will you love me, Mr. Antelope,
just the way I am?

I'm big and round,
short and fat,
and I wear a silly hat.

2

Why, no—no, I won't.
You're too big and round,
short and fat,
and I think your hat is too silly!

3

Will you love me, Mr. Baboon,
just the way I am?
I'm big and round,
short and fat,
and I wear a silly hat.

4

Why, no—no, I won't.
You're too big and round,
short and fat,
and I think your hat is too silly!

5

Will you love me, Mr. Camel,
just the way I am?
I'm big and round,
short and fat,
and I wear a silly hat.

6

Why, no—no, I won't.
You're too big and round,
short and fat,
and I think your hat is too silly!

Will you love me, Mr. Gorilla,
just the way I am?
I'm big and round,
short and fat,
and I wear a silly hat.

8

Why, no—no, I won't.
You're too big and round,
short and fat,
and I think your hat is too silly!

Will you love me, Mr. Hyena,
just the way I am?
I'm big and round,
short and fat,
and I wear a silly hat.

Why, no—no, I won't.
You're too big and round,
short and fat,
and I think your hat is too silly!

Will you love me, Mr. Lion,
just the way I am?
I'm big and round,
short and fat,
and I wear a silly hat.

Why, no—no, I won't.
You're too big and round,
short and fat,
and I think your hat is too silly!

Will you love me, Mr. Ostrich,
just the way I am?
I'm big and round,
short and fat,
and I wear a silly hat.

Why, no—no, I won't.
You're too big and round,
short and fat,
and I think your hat is too silly!

Will you love me, Mr. Zebra,
just the way I am?
I'm big and round,
short and fat,
and I wear a silly hat.

Why, no—no, I won't.
You're too big and round,
short and fat,
and I think your hat is too silly!

17

One very sad hippo.

When they noticed how sad the hippo had become…

The antelope told the baboon, the baboon explained it to the camel, the camel confessed to the gorilla, and the gorilla informed the hyena, the hyena reported it to the lion, the lion declared it to the ostrich and he summoned the zebra.

Of course we'll love you.
You're perfect just the way you are!

Made in the USA
Las Vegas, NV
07 December 2020